D1135098

THIS BOOK IS BROUGHT TO YOU BY

FOR SUDDEN ODORS!

It's like being in a field of fresh chemica—I mean honeysuckle!

Whiff

AIR FRESHENER

CAUTION! DO NOT SPRAY NEAR OPEN FLAME OR HOT LAVA

Knocks out pet odors!

GRRRR...

Hides Uncle Frank odors!

Also kills aphids and chinch bugs!

OM CHEMICAL APPEAL INDUSTRIES

TOXIC

BEFORE YOU SNIFF . . .

TAKE A **WHIFF!**

KIRK SCROGGS

SNOOP TROOP

SLOPPY JOE STINK-O-RAMA

So tender. So flavorful.

Little, Brown and Company

New York   Boston

Copyright © 2015 by Kirk Scroggs

Little, Brown and Company

Hachette Book Group
1290 Avenue of the Americas, New York, NY 10019
Visit us at lb-kids.com

Little, Brown and Company is a division of Hachette Book Group, Inc.
The Little, Brown name and logo are trademarks of Hachette Book Group, Inc.

The publisher is not responsible for websites (or their content)
that are not owned by the publisher.

First Edition: September 2015

Library of Congress Cataloging-in-Publication Data

Scroggs, Kirk.
Sloppy joe stink-o-rama / Kirk Scroggs.—First edition.
pages cm.—(Snoop Troop ; 3)
Summary: "Fifth-grade private eyes Logan and Gustavo use their doodling and detective skills to solve the mystery of a cloaked bandit who has filled their school's sloppy joe supply with stink bugs" —Provided by publisher.
ISBN 978-0-316-24278-3 (hardback)—ISBN 978-0-316-24279-0 (ebook)—
ISBN 978-0-316-36455-3 (library edition ebook) [1. Mystery and detective stories. 2. School lunchrooms, cafeterias, etc. —Fiction. 3. Schools—Fiction. 4. Humorous stories.] I. Title.
PZ7.S436726Sl 2015
[Fic]—dc23

2015012608

10 9 8 7 6 5 4 3 2

RRD-C

Printed in the United States of America

Special thanks to: Stephen Deline, Joanna Stampfel-Volpe, Jaida Temperly, Danielle Barthel, Kyle Blair-Henderson, Hiland Hall, Mark Mayes, Joe Kocian, Mamacita, Corey, Candace, Charlotte, and Isaac. And a sloppy, stinky thanks to Andrea Spooner, Deirdre Jones, Tracy Shaw, Russell Busse, and the rest of the Little, Brown crew! Woo hoo!

An Important Message from the Narrator

Hey! All you big-shot detectives!

Something's going on at the school cafeteria, and it's more disgusting than a meat-loaf-and-creamed-spinach smoothie! I need you to get over there fast and help my detectives Logan and Gustavo make sure justice is served, preferably with a nice dessert and a chocolate milk. Be sure to watch for helpful magnifying glasses like the one right here. I'd handle it myself, but I'm undercover looking for Mort Shapiro, the notorious chinchilla smuggler. That criminal coot has gotta be here somewhere!

CHAPTER 1
FREEZE, POND SCUM!

A breezy, tranquil day in Perry L. Park . . .

WELCOME TO PERRY L. PARK

PROUD HOME OF THE ARMORED DEER TICK

Kids are frolicking. . . .

Poodles are catching
Frisbees. . . .

Great gobs of sauerkraut
are being heaped on to
steaming hot dogs. . . .

The air reeks of peace and relaxation . . .

and stinky cabbage.

This is Logan Lang, founder of the Snoop Troop Detective Agency and proud member of the Student Organization of Sleuths And Detectives, or SOSAD for short.

You're right. . . . That doesn't sound nerdy at all.

So, what are you up to today, Snooper, and where's that partner of yours?

Looks like your scavenger hunt will have to wait. There are screams and splashing sounds coming from the duck pond!

Oh. It's just Logan's partner, Gustavo Muchomacho. He's been searching the pier for scavenger-hunt items, and things are going swimmingly, as in "He fell off the pier and now he's swimming."

While Logan's into Sherlock Holmes and other classic sleuths, Gustavo's all about action-movie cops with big facial hair. In fact, he's a proud member of the Whiskered Action Cop Kid Organization, or WACKO for short. He keeps his membership card on his nightstand next to his lip balm and heat-seeking Missile Mustache.

7

Speaking of Captain Mosely, I don't know about you two, but I swear I can hear his voice and the sound of police radios coming from somewhere.

Logan and Gustavo peak through the bushes
to find Captain Mosely and half the police force
surveying the grounds.

Somebody let all the residents of Murkee City Zoo out of their cages!

Wheelie is Logan's ancient, crotchety dog. His favorite foods are roast beef and pinky toes.

He's also a proud
a member of the
Canine
House **O**f **M**utts,
Pitbulls, and
Schnauzers,
also known as
CHOMPS.

Moments later, at the front gate, a strange pair of zookeepers show up with an even stranger critter.

Suddenly, a troop of untrained wombats attacks Logan and Gustavo!

Then a gigantic lion pounces in their direction! Ooh! I can't watch!

Don't worry. Wheelie's showing them who's boss.

I don't know which creature frightens me more.

GRRRR...

CHAPTER 2
TAKIN' A WHIFF

Logan, Gustavo, and the snaggle rat—I mean
Wheelie—move farther into the zoo. Faint cries
for help lead them to an old stone building
nestled in the tropical fauna: the International
House of Bugs.

I.H.O.B.
INTERNATIONAL HOUSE OF BUGS

COCOONS FOR RENT
FIRST MONTH FREE!

Keep your eyes peeled. This
place could be crawling with
clues . . . and possibly
angry scorpions.

Inside, it looks as if the bugs threw an all-night heavy metal concert. The place is ransacked.

Suddenly, a tingling sensation crawls up Logan's spine, and, surprisingly, it's not an escaped army ant. She has the distinct feeling that someone nearby needs help.

Logan's instincts are correct. There's a
disheveled zookeeper on the floor.

18

Logan whips out her pad and grills the
zookeeper like an all-beef patty.

DRAW THE SUSPECT!

Listen to Krokus's description of the suspect and sketch it on some scratch paper, the chalkboard, or any ancient Egyptian papyrus you have lying around the house.

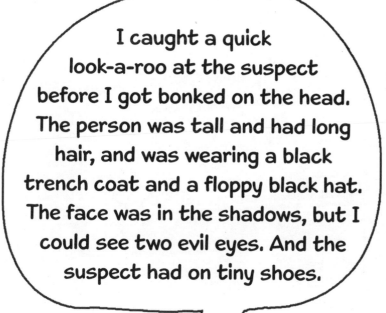

Once the interrogation is complete, Krokus bids them farewell.

On the way out, they run into a hulking hairy beast!

Don't worry. It's just Captain Mosely and his big hair. Boy, he does not look happy to see you guys.

Looks like the Snoop Troop is going to have to crack this case alone.

It's a crowded and cramped bus ride home, and like a day-old convenience-store burrito, this case doesn't sit well with Logan.

CHAPTER 3
THE CHAPTER CHAPTER

The next morning the school is abuzz with bug talk. Principal Shrub pops into Logan's class with some words of comfort.

Logan is so distracted with the zoo case, she can barely concentrate on reading, which is, like, her favorite thing in the world.

She takes notes but they are just senseless scribbles.

Even her trip to the water fountain is slightly, uh, off. . . .

SPLOOSH!

I meant to do that. My face needed a cool rinse.

Okay . . . if you say so.

At noon, she heads for the Murkee lunchroom. The joint smells of chocolate milk, and the seats are sticky with apple juice. Gustavo joins up with Logan with news of a top secret meeting.

They spot Chapster sitting at the far side of the cafeteria. He pretends not to see them.

Chapster is Logan's neighbor and an amateur cheese maker. In fact, his homemade curds won him first prize at last year's gathering of the **Y**oung **A**mericans for **C**heese **K**nowledge, also known as YACK.

Okay, kid. Time is lunch money. What have you got for us?

I present to you my latest facial-hair creation, the Shammy Stache 1260. It can absorb a hundred times its weight in liquids.

36

37

Murkee Elementary cafeteria food *is* quite repulsive. . . .

The french fries are carved from disgustingly fresh potatoes, then fried to a golden crisp and lightly dusted with sea salt.

The putrid burgers are dripping with juices from the grilled Angus beef and garden-grown tomatoes, resting under a gooey slice of melted cheddar.

And worst of all, the French artisan chefs in the kitchen sometimes accidentally put two layers of warm brownies into the ice-cream sundaes instead of the traditional one.

Wait a second!
This all sounds delicious!

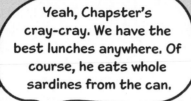

Yeah, Chapster's cray-cray. We have the best lunches anywhere. Of course, he eats whole sardines from the can.

Yummm. . . . Yes. The little fishy bones give lunch just the right crunch!

Yeah! Lunch Lady Chives is super cool. That's her having a friendly chat with Vice Principal Fudd.

40

The yelling of Lunch Lady Chives and Ms. Fudd is suddenly drowned out by even louder yelling from the lunchroom!

CHAPTER 4
YOU CAN'T KEEP A GOOD LUNCH DOWN

The dining area is a buffet of utter chaos with a side of crazy, ladled with a heaping spoonful of chopped nuts!

Okay! Enough with the bad food jokes! We've got a situation here!

Yeah! Put a fork in it! Can't you see our plates are full? There are lives at steak!

At one table, a fat and gassy stinkbug crawls out of little Nancy Tubbs's quesadilla and blasts her with a hefty dose of smell juice!

Then a stinkbug army rises up out of Nils Nargel's applesauce!

And those aren't meatballs in Finn Finnergan's spaghetti!

The whole joint is exploding with stinkbugs!

Logan spots Old Man Murray, the janitor, out in the hall with his trusty vacuum.

Logan goes wild with the vacuum!

She sucks the stinkbugs right off one kid's noggin!

Then she uses the wet-vac attachment to slurp the critters out of Chapster's mouth!

Don't eat that!

ORDER NOW!

And notice how she uses the swivel brush to sweep up pesky pistachio shells with ease! It can all be yours for just ten payments of $19.95!

Wow! I have to say you made quick work of those stinkbugs. Who knew a vacuum cleaner could be such a powerful self-defense device?

Captain Mosely swoops in and handcuffs Lunch Lady Chives!

With only a few minutes remaining until lunch period is over, Logan and Gustavo decide to sweep the kitchen for clues.

I don't know, guys. I'm not so certain the lunch lady is innocent.

CHAPTER 5

THE STACHE STASH

4:30 PM. Snoop Troop headquarters. Inside this old ice-cream truck, top forensic experts are poring over important evidence and running advanced tests. . . .

Actually, it's just Logan and Gustavo working like mad scientists trying to determine the nature of the mystery sauce absorbed into the Shammy Stache 1260.

Tests are performed.

Sauce manuals are consulted.

Ultimately, the slurp test proves most effective.

Yum! It's just sloppy joe sauce! Tangy, too!

Uh... first off, gross. Second, what is sloppy joe sauce doing in the school kitchen? Chives swore to Ms. Fudd she'd never serve it.

SLURP.

55

On the news, Lunch Lady Chives pleads her innocence from a jail cell.

In case you haven't noticed, Gustavo is kind of obsessed with fake mustaches. He has one for every occasion.

The Swiss Army Stache

The Binocu-Stache 100X

The Belgian Self-grooming Stache

The Milk Mustache
(Dispenses 2% and Chocolate)

What is it with you and mustaches?

All the great private eyes have them: Detective PJ Pantz, Hercule Poirot, Nancy Drew.

CHAPTER 6
LOCK HER UP AND THROW AWAY THE QUICHE

The Salisbury State Institute for Deranged Lunch Ladies. This place is more fortified than a balanced breakfast. They even have killer guard frogs.

Watch for guard frogs!

Hundreds of the world's most dangerous lunch ladies are locked up inside. . . .

DANGER!

Fiona Flapjack is serving ten years for giving rat nuggets to third-graders.

Betty Bunt is serving three years for egg battery and stealing twenty pounds of flour.

Yeah, I stole it. I kneaded the dough!

Try it. You'll like it.

And Bridgett Boudin is currently serving canned pears with little globs of cottage cheese.

Yep, this place is crawling with diabolical criminals

Luckily, it's Bring Your Kids to Work Day for the guards and staff!

I gotta admit, that was an ingenious plan, you guys.

While Gustavo struggles to free himself from the trash can that's been dumped over his head, Logan ventures into the dark corridors.

She keeps her eyes peeled for any crazed lunch
ladies who may have escaped their cells.

They find Lunch Lady Chives in a frantic state.

Logan asks her if she remembers anything that could help them find out who really put the stinkbugs in the school lunch.

As they leave the building, they're shocked to find the press waiting with cameras and microphones!

It's Elektra Cash and Li-Wei Chu, members of the Murkee Elementary Journalism Club. They'll do anything for a good news story . . . or a bad one.

When they get back to the ice-cream truck, they find some scoundrel has vandalized it!

Things are even worse inside!

Sounds like you really enjoyed it.

71

CHAPTER 7
GAG ME WITH A SPOON

The next day at school, Logan and Gustavo sneak into the kitchen before lunch period to search for the hidden camera Lunch Lady Chives told them about.

Find the camera!

Logan attempts to find the footage from the day of the stinkbug fiasco.

74

It's shakier and fuzzier than a ginger ale in a moon bounce. Plus, there only seems to be one usable freeze-frame of Miss Fudd in the kitchen doing some kind of inspection.

Suddenly, Logan and Gustavo get the creeping sensation that someone is lurking behind them.

Slowly, they turn to find . . .

No, that's not a mummified Aztec poodle! It's the new lunch lady!

79

Elektra and Li-Wei have a school website, but it's more like a trashy gossip page.

We gotta solve this case before the press tips off all the suspects. If only we could get hit with some new info!

Logan unfolds the paper airplane that nailed Gustavo's noggin and discovers it's actually a note. And it's in code!

Solve the pictogram!

CHAPTER 8
THE ROOT BEER OF ALL EVIL

Back at headquarters, Logan studies a map of Murkee City while Gustavo practices his Guatemalan Gator Mega Kick on a watermelon.

The map isn't clearly marked, so she searches inch by inch for the root beer bottling plant.

It's gotta be here somewhere.

I don't know if it's such a good idea for you kids to go out to that factory, alone, at night.

Narrator dude is right. We're only fourth-graders.

Yeah. You have to wait until fifth grade to get that kind of freedom. And I hear i sixth grade, you get to ride motorcycles.

Luckily, Logan's mom is available to chaperone, though she'll take some convincing. That's her in the eyepatch.

So anyway, our report on root beer is due Monday, so we have to get over to the factory pronto to interview Mr. . . . uh, Muggsly, the root beer expert.

Mmm-hmmm.

Logan's mom is the strong, silent type. She comes from a long line of ice-cream women.

Logan's Grandmother

Logan's Great-Grandmother

Logan's Great-Great-Grandmother

Logan's Great-Great-Great-Great-Great-Great-Great-Great-Great-Great-Great-Great-Great-Great-Great-Great- . . . whew! . . . Great-Great-Great-Great-Great-Great-Grandmother

They arrive downtown in search of the Froth Root Beer Plant and, lo and behold, there it is, right between Harry's Pottery and the Chamber of Commerce. The place looks pretty shady and sinister.

Inside, the factory is creakier than my uncle Mel's hip replacement. Wooden root beer barrels and vermin are everywhere. Wheelie sniffs and snorts along the floor, using his highly developed canine sense of smell to comb the place for clues.

That was an impressive burn, Gustavo, but you may have accidentally made the situation worse.

The cloaked fiend attacks, hurling
strange globs of brown goop!

Logan counters with
a Left-Foot-Out
Hokey-Pokey Kick!

Then Wheelie does
a Wheelie-Deelie
Spinout that showers
the bandit with
rocks and dirt!

But the globs keep coming!
It's too much for the Troop!

Gustavo gets beamed with a huge clump of the slop right in the kisser!

The only option is retreat!

Uh . . . I'm not so sure that's an escape portal. It looks more like a giant vat.

Suddenly, Logan gets an idea and reaches for Gustavo's face!

99

Soaked in root beer and dripping with sloppy joe, the Snoop Troop heads back to the car, where Logan's mom is waiting.

CHAPTER 9
PRESS THE MEAT

In the morning, Logan and Gustavo bike over to the one place that might be able to shed some light on the case: Slophouse Industries, the number one provider of sloppy joe filling and high cholesterol in the city.

The factory is topped with the world's second-biggest sloppy joe sandwich.

Behind closed doors, this joint is stocked with rusty machinery and conveyor belts full of chunky meat.

They dodge plenty of health-code hazards as they move through the factory looking for someone in charge.

Logan and Gustavo arrive at the office of Ms. Barbra Q. Porque. She's the seasoning specialist, sauce boss, and the meat head.

Oh, hello, children! I've been following your case on TMU News. You're investigating that funny lunch lady who doesn't believe in serving sloppy joes. Can you imagine?

Ms. Porque shows them some of her interesting experiments.

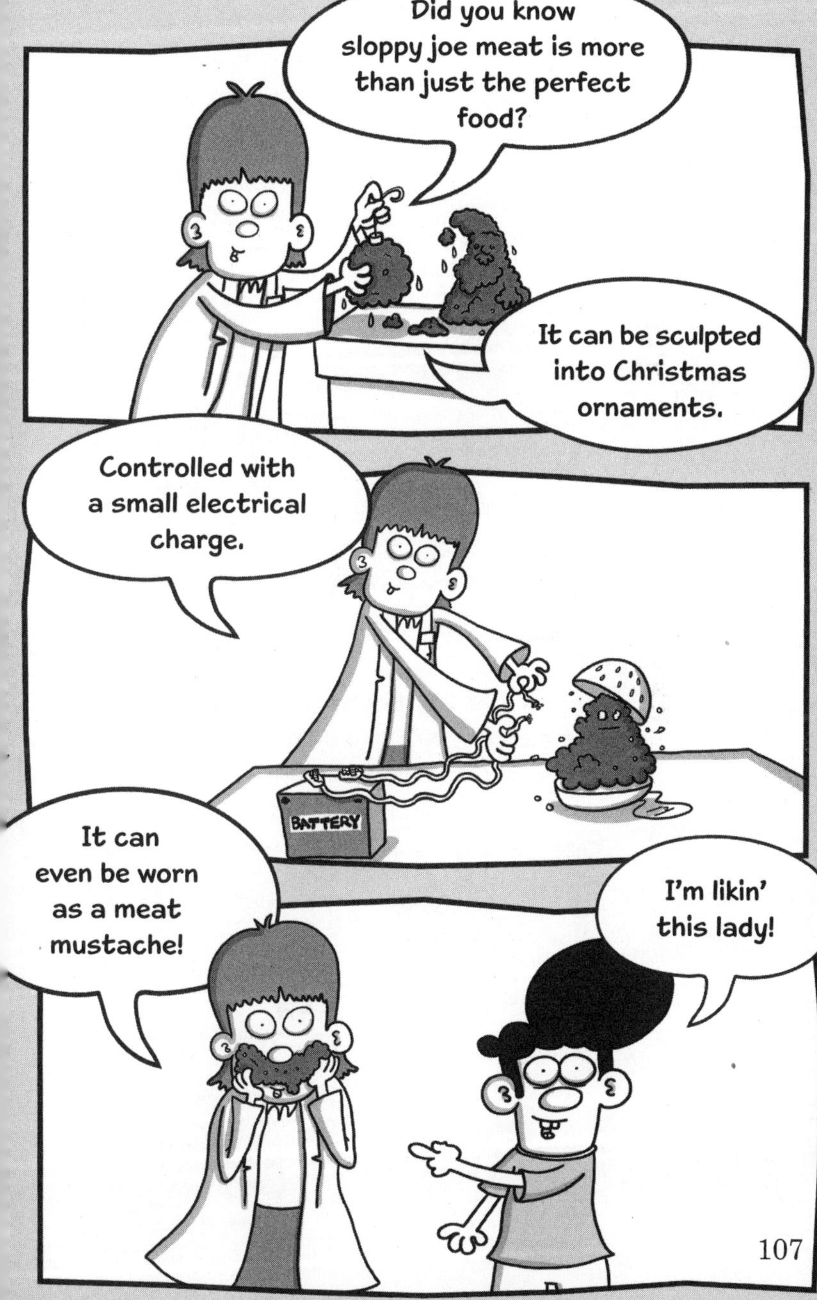

Logan and Gustavo leave Ms. Porque's office with pep in their step and BBQ sauce on their shoes.

CHAPTER 10

A SIDE OF GRILLED SUSPECTS

On her trusty dry-erase board, Logan starts to compile a list of prime suspects while Gustavo searches his smartphone for more info on stink-bugs and sloppy joes.

First stop, the International House of Bugs. They have a few more questions for Krokus, the rockin' zookeeper.

Krokus seems a little happier than the last time we saw him.

Before leaving, they check to see if Krokus has a security camera that might have footage of the theft.

We do but it's totally full of spiders, dudes.

Now I know why they call it a webcam.

They exit the bug house with very little new, helpful info.

I still can't find Lacie the flesh-eating spider! She loves snugglin' up next to toes. Rock on!

Somehow I feel even more stressed out every time I leave this place.

The Troop has to wait until Monday morning to question Ms. Fudd. They find her in her office going over the school budget. She had a very tense relationship with Lunch Lady Chives and was happy to see her go.

They grill Vera, the new lunch lady, next.

117

Logan requests a sample of Vera's sloppy joe meat.

When the bell rings, they zoom across town.

They catch Ms. Porque just in the nick of time and hand her the sample.

Ms. Porque turns on all sorts of blippy, buzzing, blinking contraptions and sticks the sloppy joe sample under a humming electron microscope.

Sorry to break the news to you, but this sloppy joe filling is different from the one you found at the root beer plant. The mystery continues.

Rats.

Look closely!

SUSPECT

Logan, you look really bummed.

All of sudden they hear a noise! Someone's following them!

Luckily, it's just Elektra and Li-Wei, disguised as garbage. They have been following the Troop, looking for a good story.

Wait a second, Troopsters. You expect these upstanding journalists to just make up stuff and pretend it's news? How dare you!

TMU News post the story right away!

The story is so big that the evening news even carries it!

CHAPTER 11
STEAK OUT

The Snoop Troop and several other hidden agents wait in the dark to see if the suspect will show up and try to steal the incriminating evidence.

You know, I never thought I'd say it, but you guys make a good duo. Such teamwork. Such friendship

Uh . . . Gustavo, speaking of shoulders— there's something on yours and it's not your BFF!

Suddenly, Chapster's voice blares out from Logan's combination lunch box/police radio!

Gustavo relays the message!

There's a cloaked figure in the yard trying to break into the ice-cream truck! What are you guys gonna do?!

Actually, it looks like someone with a powerful foot just gave the bandit the boot!

It's Logan's mom! And she's putting the serious smackdown on this creep. I think the Dallas Cowbelles oughta give her a call on draft day!

Finally, the bandit is subdued and tied to a lawn chair with a garden hose. It's time for the big reveal!

An Important Message from the Narrator

Before Logan yanks the hat off this delinquent and reveals who tried to put the smelly in school kids' bellies, let's see if you can figure out who did it first. Go back and peruse every page with one of these magnifying glasses on it, and then come back and show me your stuff. Maybe you've got what it takes to be a Snoop Trooper!

Which one of these upstanding citizens has a stinky and sloppy dark side?

 **Lunch Lady Chives** Is she guilty after all?

 **Vera the Lunch Lady** She wants Lunch Lady Chives's job, that's for sure.

 **Ms. Barbra Q. Porque** She has all kinds of access to sloppy joe ingredients.

 **Vice Principal Fudd** She was furious at Lunch Lady Chives for spending so much money on food.

 **Krokus Rattwinger** He'd do anything to promote his rock band, bro!

Turn the page for the hard-hitting truth!

Logan pulls off the hat to reveal . . .

137

What about Vice Principal Fudd? She was awfully angry with Lunch Lady Chives.

And how about Vera?

But what was Barbra Q. Porque's motive?

Captain Mosely shows up to make the arrest,
but before he can cuff her . . .

. . . the ground starts to wiggle, jiggle, and rumble!

Surprisingly, the Sloppy Joe XXL throws Ms. Porque into the air like a bucking bronco!

Uh-oh.

The beast oozes over the city like a chunky meat blanket!

144

Logan tries out her Mandarin Marinated Pork Chop Attack but her hand just squishes right through the slop!

Gustavo and Wheelie try a different strategy. . . .

And Logan's mom whips out her famous Meat Tenderizer Maneuver, but nothing seems to work!

145

Luckily, the beefy blob entangles itself in a mess of live power lines! Surely this will stop this oozing, sauce-slathered menace!

147

148

Help us find that spider before all of Murkee is slathered in BBQ sauce!

Logan grabs a leaf blower from the hardware store and blasts Lacie with a mighty gust!

Lacie gently sails through the air like a runaway kite and lands on the beefy beast.

The spider bite instantly dissolves the Sloppy Joe XXL into nothing but a pool of tangy sauce!

Well, this is a kid's book. We have to show some restraint.

CHAPTER 12
JUSTICE DESSERTS

The next day at school, the entire student body cheers Lunch Lady Chives's return to the cafeteria . . . well, everyone except Chapster and Ms. Fudd.

Unfortunately, the joy is shattered like a brittle cafeteria plate when she announces . . .

Oh, well. At least Vera agrees to bring in some healthier dining options. . . .

Lacie the pink recluse is returned to her proper home. . . .

And Logan and Gustavo reach an important agreement . . .

But, in a nearby seat, Chapster gets a strange feeling. A cold breeze blows through his bowl hairdo. There's an unwelcome presence amongst them. Something evil. Something supernatural!

DOODLE SNOOPS

CLASSIFIED

Warning: The following pages involve extreme doodling, clue finding, and pancake flipping!

Don't be drawing in this book if it doesnt belong to you or I'll have to handcuff you to a rabid platypus!

HOW TO DRAW
A STINKBUG

1. Draw a big fat booty, like a hot dinner roll.

2. Then draw some eyes, like two tiny pearls.

3. Let's add a snappy jaw, like a pair of pliers.

4. Slap some hairy legs on that sucker! Don't forget, insects have six legs, arachnids have eight, and third-graders have sixteen!

5. Put some snappy sneakers on those gams!

6. Add a blast of fresh stink juice and stand back!

Visit lb-kids.com to print out these activities.

HOW TO DRAW A SLOPPY JOE

1. First, draw some parenthesis, only turned on their side.

2. Then add some sesame seeds, like a bad case of dandruff.

3. Now it's time for the BBQ meat filling. Oh, man, this is making me hungry.

4. Let's put on a happy face!

5. And what's a sloppy joe without a delicious beverage?

6. Make sure you serve it on an elderly tortoise's shell—this is customary in most countries except for Sweden.

HOW TO DRAW A LUNCH LADY

1. Start with two eyes, like a couple of slices of pepperoni.

2. Add a cute nose and a wrinkly mouth and chin below it.

3. Make sure her hair is as poofy as some fresh blue-raspberry cotton candy.

4. Don't foget the charming hat, lacy collar, and earrings shaped like a chicken drumstick. A girl's gotta have her accessories!

5. Plus a stylish apron straight from the fashion runways of Milan!

6. And top it off with a heaping spoonful of steaming monkey brains. Lunch is served!

Visit lb-kids.com to print out these activities.

HOW TO DRAW DETECTIVE P.J. PANTZ

1. Begin with two squares with fuzzy things on top. These are some cool shades and bushy brows.

2. Next, add a manly schnozz with some serious stache growing out of it like a tropical fern.

3. Then add a stylin' do, like a porcupine that's fallen into a vat of hair gel.

4. Don't forget the necktie and a whiskered chin, like a freshly shorn sheep.

5. A cop's gotta have a badge!

6. And lastly, his favorite PJ's—the ones with Captain Panther Man on them. He also likes the ones with little teddy bears on them, but don't tell anyone.

It's nap time, punk!

What's in Wheelie's bowl and why is it wriggling?

Visit lb-kids.com to print out these activities.

MUSTACHE ART

CREATE YOUR OWN HI-TECH CRUMB CATCHER

Be sure and include lots of mayonnaise and golden raisins!

Some beast broke into the insect exhibit, and now half the army ants have gone AWOL! Help us catch the criminal before any more bugs go bye-bye!

- It was hairy.

- It was about as big as a raccoon.

- It had a looong snout.

- It had four legs and pointy ears.

- It had a three-foot-long tongue as skinny as a piece of strawberry licorice lace.

Visit lb-kids.com to print out this activity.

The local arcade has been invaded by stinkbugs!

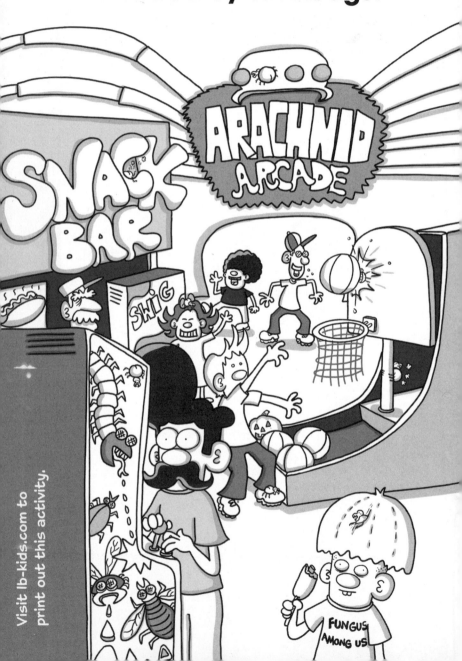

Barbra Q. Porque needs a fresh batch of sloppy joe filling. Draw in the ingredients and send them through the meat grinder. Don't forget the rhubarb!

Krokus, like, totally needs your help . . . to the max, yo!

CRACKPOT

Totally Made Up News got some exclusive photos of the Sloppy Joe XXL attack but something looks a little fishy about that second pic.

Visit lb-kids.com to print out this activity.

SNAPSHOT

Find the differences between the two images before they get posted online. The answers are on the next page. Anyone caught cheating gets a stinkbug in each nostril!

Visit lb-kids.com to print out these activities.

WORD SEARCH

M	P	L	I	C	W	O	L	S	S	I	N	S	E	C	T	S
U	E	S	C	Y	T	Q	V	W	T	G	I	N	C	A	S	L
S	W	G	O	L	H	T	C	I	I	R	T	L	H	L	W	O
H	D	A	I	B	P	H	F	I	N	U	R	O	A	C	H	P
E	R	O	O	T	B	E	E	R	K	B	S	G	P	L	Y	P
R	I	W	U	Y	H	F	K	B	B	W	P	A	S	C	E	Y
Y	U	E	S	O	S	T	A	A	U	O	I	N	T	R	N	J
S	T	I	N	K	Y	S	D	L	G	R	D	R	E	F	A	O
Z	O	O	N	L	P	W	B	L	B	M	E	J	R	T	S	E
M	Y	S	T	E	R	Y	M	E	A	T	R	T	U	P	I	S

Hey, rookie! Help us find any words related to bugs, smells, and Vera's delicious cooking!

Answers on the next page!

DOODLE SNOOPS ANSWER KEY

WORD SEARCH:

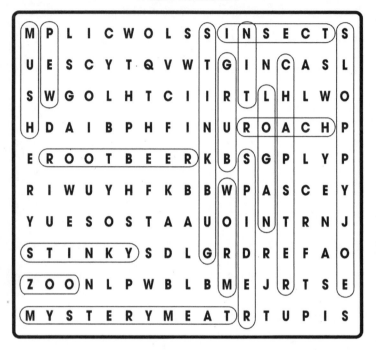

KIRK SCROGGS

is the author and illustrator of *Snoop Troop: It Came from Beneath the Playground*, *Snoop Troop: Attack of the Ninja Potato Clones*, the Tales of a Sixth-Grade Muppet series, and the Wiley & Grampa's Creature Features series. He lives in Los Angeles.